Copyright © 2020 T. Troy Kolo.

All rights reserved.

ISBN: 9798577551599

Rockefeller,
The Christmas Owl

It was a typical afternoon...

That is, if you're an owl like me.
Let me restate that,
an owl like me.
I was perched on a branch
of a green piney tree.
Looking out towards the meadow,
the view before me.
Surveying our lot with grasses and leaves.
Living here with my parents,
quite comfortably.

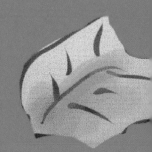

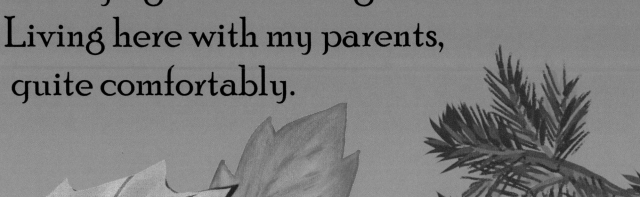

When whoosh! Came a wind
quite sudden and strong.

It wasn't at all like summer or autumn,
But mother and father
have told me this often.
For father is wise and has stories to tell,
He teaches me things
for keeping me well.

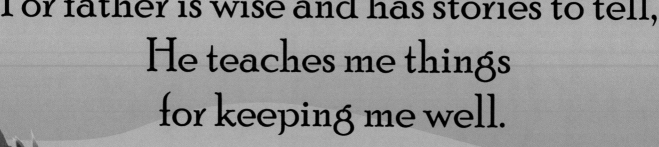

Mother she gathers up snacks I like best,
Bringing them back to eat at our nest.

That strong gust of wind
came once again,
And that was the signal
for me to go in.

I had just found something
that was shiny and flat,
And brought it up here
to the branch where I sat.

Sometimes people would
drop things on the ground,
For me to find them
to bring them around.

I like to go fetch things,
as that's my employ,
that sparkle and shimmer
which mother enjoys.
Then place them around
to adorn our nest,
It brightens our spirits
and brings happiness.

Now father would tell me
"Use grasses and twigs,
These, are what makes for a nest to grow big."
Now over the branches I hop on my feet,
Thinking of what I might find there to eat.

When just then a rush of men under our tree,
Startled my mother and father and me.
Father and mother owl
flew off just then,
Expecting that I would
be following.

Afraid at
that moment,
too nervous
to move,

Alone in my house.
What should I do?
Meaning no harm
as these weren't bad men,
They just didn't notice the nest there within.
Just then a loud rumble, the sound of a saw,
As the engine and chain started to gnaw.

Rrrrr, Rrrrr, Rrrrr!
Rrrrr!

The workers below were sawing our tree!

It swayed this way and that way
and started to lean,
It toppled right over,
and fell to the ground.

Bang, splat! It was flat,
Came down, quick as that!

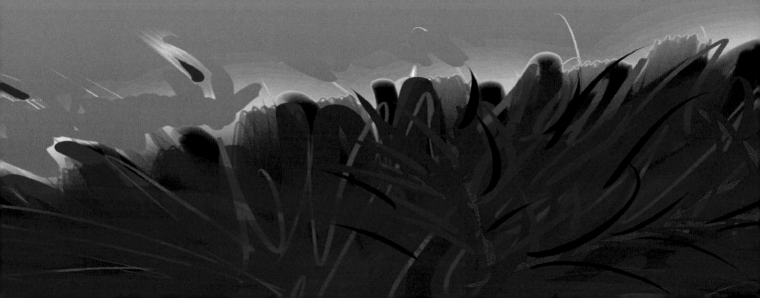

No worry for me as I flew from the tree,

The place we call home for my family.
By the side of the meadow
perched up above,
Awaiting my parents
for whom I do love.

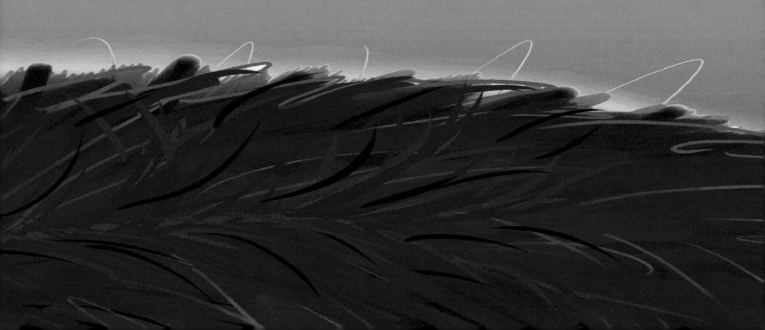

Nightfall was coming, no sign of my folks.
Across on the meadow the workers I note.
The tree they were tying
  for hauling away,
Down to the city
  for Christmas display?

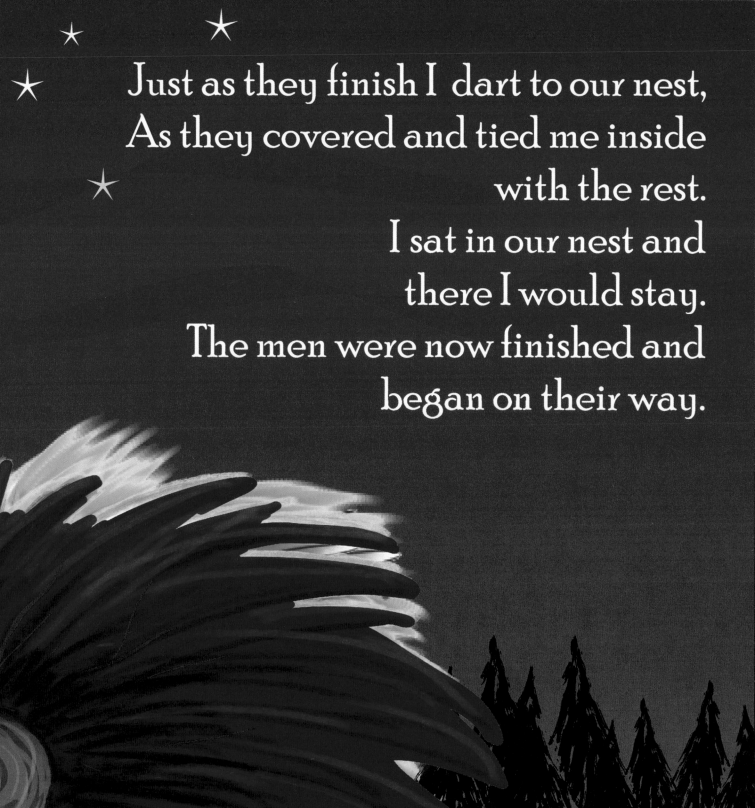

Just as they finish I dart to our nest,
As they covered and tied me inside
with the rest.
I sat in our nest and
there I would stay.
The men were now finished and
began on their way.

Day one
 and day two, then the third day had come,
Of travel by trailer in tree was no fun.
No food and no water,
 just where were we going?
Now that we're here,
 where had we come?

The cars with their horns
and the noises and sounds.
As all of the people
they shuffle around.
Soon up goes my tree,
Well how can this be?

As the branches unfold I sigh with relief.
I'm no longer trapped in our nest,
thankfully!

The first thing
I notice.
The first
thing
I see.

The city
with
buildings
much
taller
than
trees.

Looking below was a pond
that was froze,
Some people
were skating around
as they go.

Nearest a statue
it gleaming of gold,
Each way that I looked
was a sight to behold.

There's angels
with trumpets
that sparkle
and shine.

Nothing before
have I ever
seen finer.

With flashes of light that twinkle and glow.
But,

Just then I remember my parents still gone.
How would I find them now on my own?

I cried to the workmen as to where I had come.
But none of them answered, as most people do,
They don't speak owl and haven't a clue.

There's pigeons below me
I'll ask some of them,
Maybe they'll tell me just where to begin.
One said
"That man in the red suit travels up north,
Perhaps he can help you to locate them both."

I flew down right next to the man in the chair,
and listened as children requested their wares.
Telling him just what they want
and would like,
One wants a dolly
the other a bike.

I wanted something that couldn't be brought,
So maybe I can't ask, was my first thought.
I picked up some tinsel,
flew back to the tree,
To make it most festive
and to comfort me.

For days and days
I'd wait and worry
before my spirit falls
lets hurry

For days
I would think of just how to get back.
Then Santa came past me, peddling his pack.
I asked him to help me
to find my way home.
To get to my parents,
I'm here all alone.

I can't get back by the way I had come.

As Santa was softly humming a song. Said,
"Of course I can help you! Just follow along,
I'm sure I'll glide past them
this Christmas Eve night,
I make all my rounds
by reindeer sleigh flight.

Just follow here with me
if you can
squeeze
in.

My
to all

sleigh's full of presents this season of giving,
the good children these toys I'm delivering."

As Santa fills stockings,
I decorate trees.
I fly down the chimneys,
quick as a breeze,
at each of the houses
on Christmas Eve.

Then, Rocke spied something familiar to him.
A glimpse of the meadow and there was his kin.
Imagine my joy!
Upon seeing them.
There's mom and my dad! Can it really be them?

Yes, wishes can come true.
I'm here, home again.
In time for Christmas.
Bless us, Amen.

My Own Holiday Memories:

(write in space below)

This book is dedicated to
my mother and grandmother whom
always made the Christmas holidays special.

Written by T. Troy Kolo.

With Illustrations by Meredith Miner

Design and Layout T. Troy Kolo.

To contact the author
email to: rocke.owl@gmail.com

Copyright © 2020 T. Troy Kolo.

All rights reserved.

ISBN: 9798577551599